For Dad

&

new Dad

ATHENEUM BOOKS FOR YOUNG READERS
An imprint of Simon & Schuster Children's
Publishing Division
1230 Avenue of the Americas,
New York, New York 10020
Copyright © 2011 by Elanna Allen
All rights reserved, including the right of
reproduction in whole or in part in any form.
ATHENEUM BOOKS FOR YOUNG READERS is a
registered trademark of Simon & Schuster, Inc.
For information about special discounts
for bulk purchases, please contact Simon &
Schuster Special Sales at 1-866-506-1949 or
business@simonandschuster.com.
The Simon & Schuster Speakers Bureau can
bring authors to your live event. For more
information or to book an event, contact
the Simon & Schuster Speakers Bureau at
1-866-248-3049 or visit our website at
www.simonspeakers.com.
Book design by Ann Bobco
The text for this book is set in
ITC American Typewriter Medium.
The illustrations for this book are rendered
in pencil with digital color.
Manufactured in the United States of America
0411 PCR

2 4 6 8 10 9 7 5 3
Library of Congress Cataloging-in-Publication Data
Allen, Elanna.
Itsy Mitsy runs away / Elanna Allen.
— 1st ed.
p. cm.
Summary: When a little girl decides to run away,
her father helps her pack.
ISBN 978-1-4424-0671-1 (hardcover)
[1. Runaways—Fiction. 2. Fathers and
daughters—Fiction. 3. Humorous stories.] I. Title.
PZ7.A42555It 2011
[E]—dc22
2010004418

ITSY MITSY runs away

by ELANNA ALLEN

Atheneum Books for Young Readers

New York London Toronto Sydney

Have you met Itsy Mitsy?

She's
the little girl who
really,
really,
for real
(I'm not even joking)
doesn't like . . .

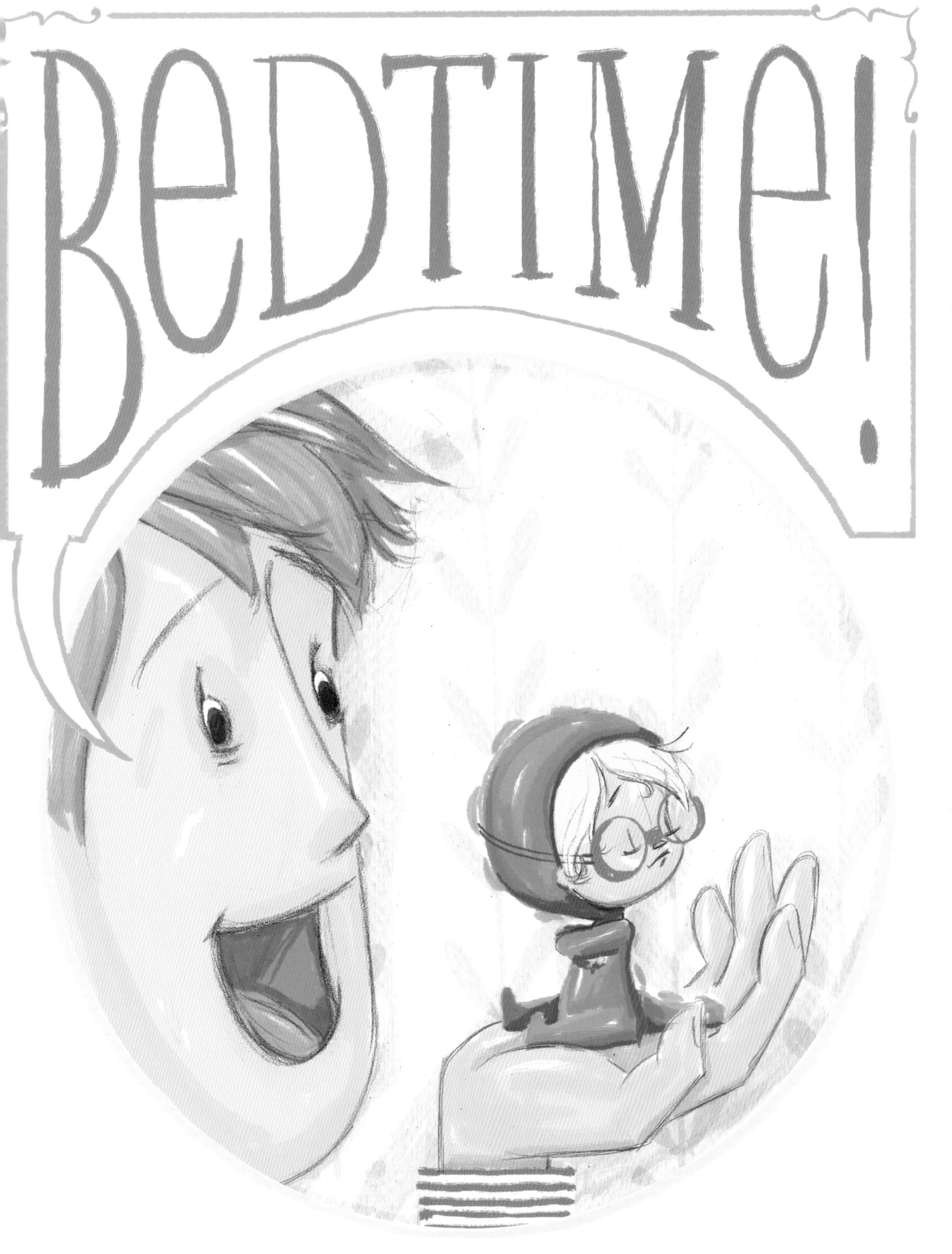
BEDTIME!

So she decided to run away.

"If you're going to
run away from me,"
Dad sniffed,
"then at least let me
help you pack.

For starts,
you'll need a friend.
No bedtime is one thing—
but no friends?
That's too much."

So Mitsy packed her friendliest dinosaur, Mister Roar, and said,

GOOD-BYE.
I'M RUNNING away.

"Okay! Bye!" Dad called, and then added, "What will Mister Roar eat when he gets hungry?"

Mitsy stopped in her tracks.

"Good point.
Dinosaurs do like
to nibble,"
she said
as she searched
the fridge.

Mitsy packed a small snack for Mister Roar and yelled,

ALL PACKED!
I'M RUNNING AWAY.

"Oh!" said Dad.

"Mister Roar likes bananas?

So do the bedtime beasties!

Perhaps you'll see one!

Do send a photo."

BEDTIME
BEASTIES?

Mitsy froze.

"Mm, maybe pack something to shoo them off," suggested Dad.

So Mitsy packed her ferocious dog, Puptart.

HE'LL BARK AT THE BEASTS

TO GUARD THE SNACK THAT I JUST PACKED

FOR MY FRIENDLIEST DINOSAUR, MISTER ROAR!

NOW I'M RUNNING AWAY.

"You've packed Puptart?
Good thinking!" cried Dad.
"Beasties would be scared of dogs . . .
if they could see in the dark."

"I have just the thing,"
answered Mitsy,
who, indeed,
had *just* the thing.

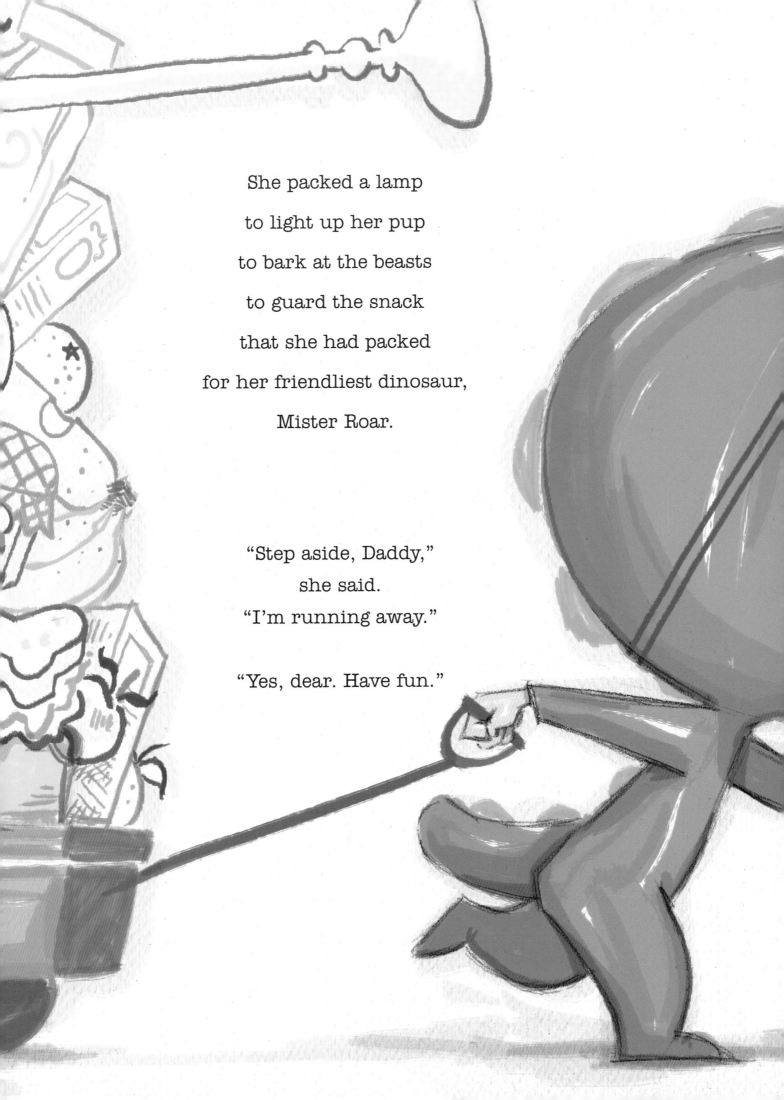

She packed a lamp
to light up her pup
to bark at the beasts
to guard the snack
that she had packed
for her friendliest dinosaur,
Mister Roar.

"Step aside, Daddy,"
she said.
"I'm running away."

"Yes, dear. Have fun."

"Oh!" Dad called after her.
"Do they have outlets where you're going?
To plug things like lamps in?"

But try as she might, Mitsy couldn't take the outlet out of the wall,

or the wall out of the house.

So she did the only sensible thing she could think of.

She packed

the whole house

to plug in the lamp

to light up her pup

to bark at the beasts

to guard the snack

that Mitsy had packed

for her friendliest dinosaur,

Mister Roar.

THaT
SHOULD DO It!
I'M (erg) rUNNiNG
(oof) awaY!

"Have a nice trip,
dear!"
cried Dad.
"And don't forget
to mow
the lawn!"

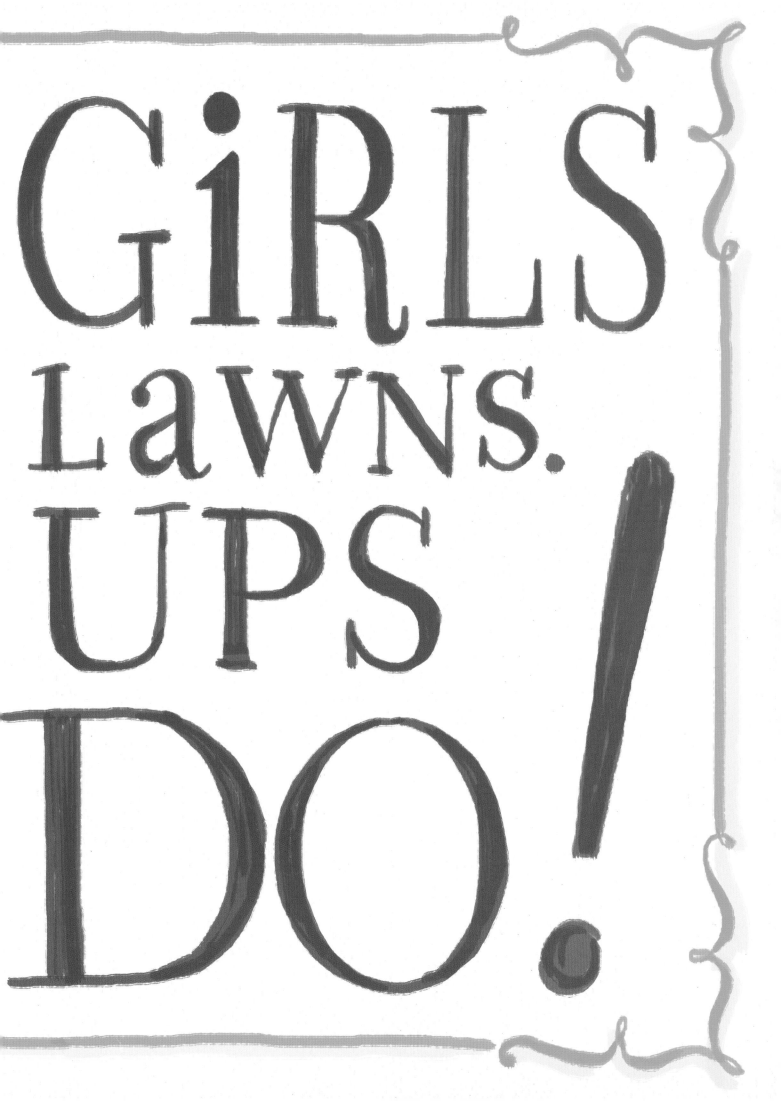

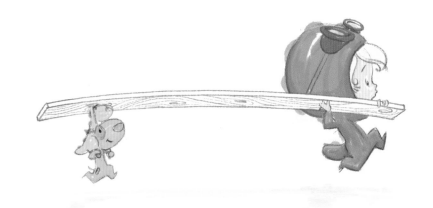

So she packed her dad

to mow the lawn

around the house

that held the lamp

that lit up her pup

who barked at the beasts

to guard the snack

that Mitsy had packed

for her friendliest dinosaur,

Mister Roar.

And then . . .

Itsy Mitsy ran away.

Soon Itsy Mitsy
found the perfect place
where there was
no bedtime ever,
not even one.

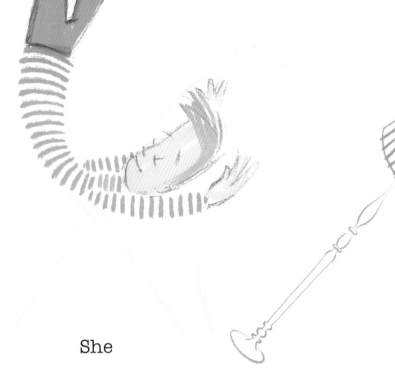

She

unpacked her dad

to mow the lawn

around the house

that held the lamp

that lit up her pup

who barked at the beasts

to guard the snack

that Mitsy had packed

for her friendliest dinosaur,

Mister Roar,

and then she let out a little . . .

Good thing Dad was there to tuck her in.